MACMILLAN
INTERMEDIA

D1151366

STEPHEN KING

The Girl Who Loved Tom Gordon

Retold by John Escott

MACMILLAN

Founding Editor: John Milne

The Macmillan Readers provide a choice of enjoyable reading materials for learners of English. The series is published at six levels – Starter, Beginner, Elementary, Pre-intermediate, Intermediate and Upper.

Level control

Information, structure and vocabulary are controlled to suit the students' ability at each level.

The number of words at each level:

Starter	about 300 basic words
Beginner	about 600 basic words
Elementary	about 1100 basic words
Pre-intermediate	about 1400 basic words
Intermediate	about 1600 basic words
Upper	about 2200 basic words

Vocabulary

Some difficult words and phrases in this book are important for understanding the story. Some of these words are explained in the story and some are shown in the pictures. From Pre-intermediate level upwards, words are marked with a number like this: ...³. These words are explained in the Glossary at the end of the book.

Contents

A Note About the Author

Stephen Edwin King is a famous American writer of stories of horror and suspense. He was born in 1947, in Portland, in the state of Maine. His ancestors came to the U.S.A. from Scotland and Ireland.

Stephen King attended several schools in Maine, and then completed his education at the University of Maine at Orono. Stephen began his career as a writer at the university, contributing a weekly article to the student newspaper. He also met his wife, Tabitha, at Orono, where she was a student. Stephen and Tabitha were married in 1971. They have three children.

When he finished college, Stephen King became a teacher, but he wrote stories in the evenings and on weekends. Many of these stories were published in well-known magazines.

Stephen King finished his first novel, *Carrie*, in 1973, and it was published the following year. The book became very popular, and Stephen was soon able to stop teaching and start writing full-time. His next two novels, *Salem's Lot* (1975) and *The Shining* (1978), also became very popular and, like *Carrie* and many of his later stories such as *Christine* (1983), *Misery* (1987) and *The Green Mile* (1996), they were made into successful films. Stephen King is now one of the world's best known writers.

The Girl Who Loved Tom Gordon was first published in 1999.

A Note About This Story

The main character in the story, Trisha McFarland, is a nine-year-old girl who loves watching the game of baseball. Baseball is one of the most popular sports in North America. Trisha is a fan of a famous baseball team, the Boston Red Sox, and her favorite player is Tom Gordon. Although the story is not a true one, the Boston Red Sox is a real team and Tom Gordon played for this team between 1996 and 1999.

The reader does not need to know all the rules of baseball to understand the story. But some special baseball words are used, so here is a short description of the game. Two teams compete in a game of baseball. They *bat* and *field* alternately. A game is divided into nine sections—*innings*. Each team both bats and fields during an inning. A player from the fielding team throws—*pitches*—the ball at a *batter* from the other team. The batter tries to hit the ball with his bat. The *pitcher* stands on a slightly raised area of the ground called the *mound*. The batter stands beside a flat piece of rubber called the *home plate*. The batter can score *runs* by hitting the ball and running between a number of places on the field called *bases*. If the batter does not hit a ball which passes over the home plate, this is called a *strike*. After three strikes, the batter is *out*, and is replaced by another batting player from his team. After three batters are out, half an inning is over and the batting team becomes the fielding team. The team which has scored the most runs by the end of the ninth inning wins the game. Each year, the best teams in the U.S.—the major leagues—compete in the World Series.

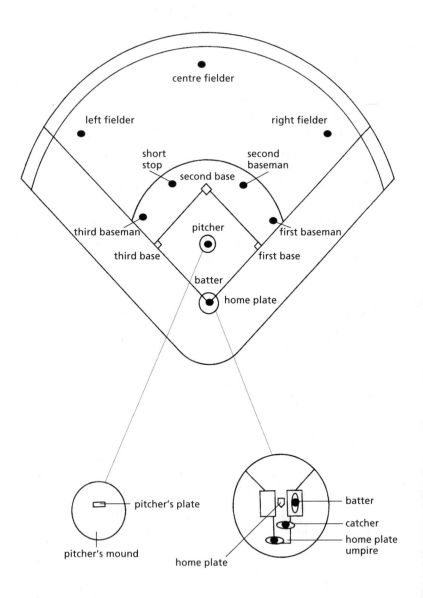

centre fielder

left fielder   right fielder

short
stop   second
baseman
second base

third baseman   first baseman

pitcher

third base   first base

batter

home plate

pitcher's plate

pitcher's mound

batter

catcher

home plate
umpire

home plate

A baseball bat

A pitcher's glove

A baseball

A batter

A pitcher

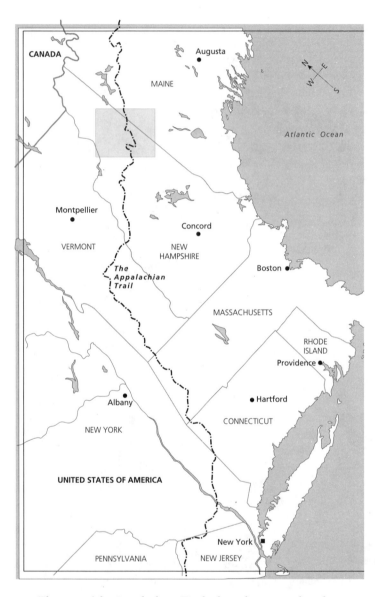

The part of the Appalachian Trail where this story takes place

1

Trisha

At ten o'clock on a Saturday morning in early June, Trisha McFarland was sitting in the back seat of her mother's car. She was playing with Mona, her doll.

Trisha was nine years old. That morning, she was wearing her blue baseball cap and her Red Sox baseball jersey. The jersey had 36 GORDON printed on the back.

At ten o'clock, Trisha was playing safely with Mona in her mother's car. Half an hour later, she was lost in the woods.

How did this happen?

"It happened because I needed to pee[1]," Trisha thought angrily. "Why didn't I ask Pete and Mother to wait while I peed behind a tree? I was stupid!"

But Trisha hadn't wanted to talk to her mother or her brother, Pete. Pete and his mother had been arguing again. Trisha hated their arguments. She was tired of listening to them. That morning, Trisha had wanted to scream at her mother. She had wanted to scream, "Let him go! If he wants to go back to Malden and live with Dad, let him go! Then we can get some peace and quiet!"

Pete was nearly fourteen. Pete and Trisha's mother and father had been divorced a year before. Their mother had gotten custody[2] of Pete and Trisha. She had moved from Malden, just outside Boston, to a town in southern Maine. Pete hated their new home and he also hated his new school. He wanted to live with his father.

In Malden, Pete had lots of friends. He'd been "king" of his school's computer club. At his new school, there was no computer club, and Pete had had only one friend—a boy named Eddie Rayburn. But Eddie had moved away, and now Pete was alone. And there was something worse than that. A lot of the kids at school laughed at him because he loved working with computers. They called him "Pete's CompuWorld[3]"!

On some weekends, Trisha and Pete went to Malden to be with their father. On the weekends when they didn't go to Malden, their mother usually took them out. Sometimes they went to museums, sometimes they took a canoe trip[4] on the Saco River. Sometimes they took a skiing trip. But whatever they did, Pete and his mother always argued.

This weekend, the trip was to a small town in the western part of the state. They were going to walk on a small part of the Appalachian Trail[5] which went through that area.

On the Friday night before the trip, Mom had shown Trisha and Pete a map. She'd pointed to a blue line.

"This road is Route 68," she'd said. She moved her finger a little. "We'll park the car here. This is part of the Appalachian Trail. The trail crosses Route 68 and then Route 302 in North Conway, which is in New Hampshire. It's a six mile walk." She moved her finger again. "And this is the parking lot where we come out onto Route 302. From there, a little truck will take us back to our car. Two hours later we'll be home again, and we can go to a movie. OK?"

Pete had said nothing then. But he'd had a lot to say on the trip this morning. "I don't want to do this," he'd told his mother. "It's stupid. It's going to rain later. Why do we have to walk six miles through the woods at this time of year? It's the worst time of year for bugs[6] in the woods!"

It had been a horrible journey in the car! At first, Mom

said nothing. But finally she got angry and started to shout at him.

Trisha tried not to listen to them. She took off her Red Sox baseball cap and looked at the signature written across the front of it. It was Tom Gordon's signature. Tom Gordon was Trisha's favorite Red Sox player. Her dad liked him too. Her dad liked him because Gordon stayed calm at all times. "That man has ice in his blood!" Larry McFarland often said.

Trisha had told her best friend, Pepsi Robichaud, that she thought that Tom Gordon was "quite handsome". But she often told Mona, her doll, that the man with number 36 on his jersey was the handsomest man alive!

"If he touched me, I would faint," she told the doll. "If he ever kissed me, I would probably die!"

So that morning, Trisha looked at the name on her baseball cap and tried not to listen to her mother and her brother shouting at each other. She was still looking at the cap when her mother turned the car into the parking lot.

"Kids, don't forget to put your ponchos[7] in your backpacks[8]" Mom said, looking up at the sky. "It might rain later."

There was blue sky above them, but the clouds were getting thicker in the west. It probably *would* rain soon. Pete had been right about that.

"Do you have your lunches?" Mom asked. "And do you have your bug spray? Trisha?"

"I have it, Mom," Trisha said quickly. Did she have it? She wasn't really sure. But she didn't want her mother to stop to look through her backpack. If she did that, Pete would start complaining again.

"OK, kids," Mom said. "Let's go!"

"I hate this!" Pete said.

And after only a few minutes, he and Mom were arguing again. Pete was complaining about his school and the other kids there.

"It's not easy to make friends, Peter," Mom told him. "You have to talk to the other kids. You can't just wait for them to come to you."

"You don't understand," Pete answered angrily. "School these days isn't like it was when you were young."

"I don't agree with you," Mom said.

"Those two don't even remember that I'm here," Trisha said to herself as she walked behind them.

After a while, they came to a place where the trail divided into two paths. The wider path went to the left. There was a sign next to it with the words TO NORTH CONWAY on it. The sign for the narrow path had the words TO KEZAR NOTCH.

"I have to pee!" Trisha called out. "You two go on. I'll run and catch up with you later."

Her mother and brother were shouting at each other and they didn't hear her. They walked on, up the wider path towards North Conway.

"Well, I'm going to pee," Trisha said to herself. She looked for somewhere private—a place where nobody could see her. She walked a little way down the path for Kezar Notch. Here the trees were closer together. She looked around, saw nobody, and walked off the path into the trees on the left. She could still hear her mother and brother arguing. She looked back, and she could still see the Kezar Notch path. That was good. But anyone who came along it would be able to see her. That *wasn't* good! So she went down a hill into a little ravine[9], her shoes slipping on dead leaves as she moved.

When Trisha got to the bottom of the ravine, she couldn't

"You two go on. I'll run and catch up with you later."

see the path any more. Good! And straight ahead, she could hear a man's voice and the sound of a girl laughing.

"They must be hikers[10] on the main trail—the path to North Conway," Trisha thought. "They aren't far away, so I'll soon find the trail again. But I can't see *them* and they can't see *me*."

She looked around once more, then she pulled down her jeans.

————

After Trisha had peed and pulled up her jeans, she turned around. She turned towards the little hill which she had run down. And then she turned around again. At that moment, an idea came into her head. It was the worst idea of her life! This idea was to go forward, instead of going back to the Kezar Notch path. She remembered that the two paths diverged[11] like the top of a letter Y. She would just walk across to the North Conway path.

"It's easy," she said to herself. "And it isn't far. I can't get lost."

2

Lost!

Trisha quickly climbed up the west side of the ravine. Then she started walking towards the place where the voices had come from. But there were a lot of bushes to go around, and after about ten minutes she stopped.

"Why haven't I reached the North Conway path by now?"

she thought. "I didn't go far down the Kezar Notch path. The distance between the two arms of the Y can't be this great!"

She listened for voices on the main trail, but now the woods were silent. Well, that wasn't really true. She could hear the sound of the wind in the trees. She could hear birds singing, and the buzzing sound of mosquitoes[12] around her head.

Trisha started walking forward again, and she walked faster now. Soon she came to a huge tree that had fallen to the ground. It was blocking her way. The tree was too high to climb over. The sensible thing to do was to go around it.

"But I need to go straight ahead," she said to herself. "What if I lose my way?" And she got an answer. *You've already lost your way*, a voice in her head whispered to her. It was a terrible, cold voice. She hated it!

"Shut up[13]! I have *not* lost my way!" she whispered back.

She decided to crawl under the tree, so she got down onto the ground on her hands and knees. But she got trapped by the branches of the tree. She had to take off her backpack and start again. She noticed that her hands were shaking.

"I'm not scared," she said aloud. "I'll be back on the trail in five minutes."

Pushing her backpack ahead of her, Trisha started to crawl under the tree. When she was halfway through, something suddenly moved under her. She looked down and saw a big fat black snake moving through the leaves! She screamed and tried to get up, but part of a tree branch hit her in the back. She fell down again.

She was almost crying when she crawled out from under the tree. Then she stood up and ran. She ran as fast as she

She looked down and saw a big fat black snake.

could, holding her backpack in her hand.

She looked back over her shoulder, to see if the snake was following her. As she turned, she tripped over a rock and fell heavily onto her side. This sent a pain shooting through her back, in the place where the tree branch had hit her.

Trisha lay on her side in the leaves. *Go back to the big tree where the snake is.* It was the voice inside her head again. *Then look straight ahead. That's the way to the main trail.*

But *was* it the right way? Trisha was not sure.

She walked slowly back to the fallen tree, trying not to cry. Why had she left the path? On the path she'd been safe! She felt angry with herself. And suddenly, she noticed that her back felt cold. She found that the tree branch had made a hole in her shirt, and when she put her fingers through it, she found blood on them. She closed her eyes. "I'm OK," she said to herself. "All I have to do is to stay calm. Calm like Tom Gordon. I'll hear people over on the trail in a minute or two."

She put the straps of her backpack over her shoulders again and started to walk in a straight line. Now she was walking toward a tall pine tree. There were bugs buzzing around her head. She went past the pine tree and on toward some bushes with bright red checkerberries[14] on them. Trisha knew that these berries were OK to eat, but she wasn't hungry. She walked on in a straight line to a big rock, then past the rock and halfway up a small hill. Then she stopped.

There were bugs all around her. The mosquitoes were buzzing around her ears. She dropped her backpack onto the ground and opened it. Inside it she found her blue plastic poncho, her lunch, some suntan lotion[15], a bottle of water, a bottle of soda, some Twinkies[16] and a bag of potato chips.

17

But no bug spray!

There was no bug spray, so Trisha rubbed some of the suntan lotion on her skin. Maybe it would keep the bugs away. Then she put everything back into her pack. She looked at the Twinkies for a moment, but she still wasn't hungry.

"I won't eat yet," she said to herself.

No, not yet, said the voice in her head. *But you might never get out of these woods.*

"Shut up! Shut up! Shut up!" she told the voice.

Trees moved in the wind, mosquitoes buzzed, and Trisha could hear a plane far away. But there were no voices from a nearby path.

Her legs and stomach both felt heavy. But her head felt light and strange.

It was then that Trisha started to cry, and the words came screaming out of her mouth.

"Help me, I'm lost! Please help me, I'm lost!"

Yes, she was lost!

3

The Radio

Trisha shouted and screamed for about fifteen minutes. Then she sat down beside her pack and cried. When at last she stopped, she felt a little better—except for the bugs. The bugs were everywhere, buzzing and crawling and trying to drink her blood. Trisha got up and waved her Red Sox cap at them to push them away.

As she started to walk again, she saw six or seven mosquitoes on her arm. She hit them angrily, killing three of
them. Two had been full of her blood, and when she saw the
blood on her arm, she felt weak and sick. She had to sit
down again. She cried for another minute or two. Then she
got up, feeling calmer.

She thought about Pete and her mother.

"They'll know that I'm lost by now," she told herself.
"They'll call out my name. If they don't hear me, they'll go
back along the trail. They'll ask people if they've seen a girl
with a Red Sox cap. And when they get back to the car and
find that I'm not there, they'll get worried. Mom will be
frightened."

The thought of Mom being frightened made Trisha feel
unhappy as well as afraid. There were going to be lots of
people looking for her—game wardens and people from the
Forest Service[17]. She began to walk faster. She was hoping to
get back to the main trail before all this started to happen.

Trisha would have been shocked to know that, at that
moment, her mother and brother hadn't realized that she
was lost. They were still arguing and they had not noticed
that she wasn't with them!

———

Trisha walked faster and faster, listening and calling, calling
and listening. But soon, she wasn't really listening any more.
And when she began to run, she did it without knowing
what she was doing. Trees and bushes scratched her arms
and her face, and made holes in her jeans, but she didn't
notice what was happening.

She ran up a hill, jumping over some small trees which

had fallen in a long-ago storm. At the top of the hill, she looked down and saw a long blue-gray valley below her. There was a steep cliff in front of her feet. More steep cliffs rose up miles away on the far side of the valley.

Suddenly, Trisha imagined herself falling over the edge of the cliff, screaming for her mother. But she turned quickly and she ran along the hilltop until she reached a fallen tree. Trisha fell onto it and put her arms round it, shaking from head to foot. Again, she imagined herself falling.

"No!" she screamed. Then spoke more quietly. "I'm all right. I'm OK, I'm OK."

She said the words again and again, but it was three minutes before she could move away from the tree and look out across the valley again. She saw rain clouds in the sky now. She saw lots of trees. But no people. Not even smoke from a camp fire. There was no one nearby.

"But I'm OK," she told herself again.

She stepped away from the tree and screamed again as something touched the backs of her legs. Were there more snakes here? She turned, but there were no snakes. There were only bushes—checkerberry bushes. And now the bugs had found her again and they were dancing around her eyes. And now the insects were getting bigger and bigger!

"I'm fainting, I'm fainting," she thought before her eyes closed and she fell back into the bushes. In a moment she was unconscious and after another moment or two the mosquitoes began to feed on her face and eyelids.

———

Something cold fell onto Trisha's nose, and she opened her eyes. More water fell onto her face, and a crash of thunder came from above her. Trisha gave a little scream as the rain

There was no one nearby.

started to fall hard and fast. Lightning hit a half-dead tree on the valley floor below her, and she saw the tree explode into two pieces.

She ran back into the woods, opened her pack and got out her poncho. She put it on and sat on a fallen tree. Her eyelids felt swollen and itchy. She listened to the rain falling and watched a cloud of bugs dancing in front of her. "Nothing makes them go away and they're always hungry," she thought. "They fed on my eyelids when I was unconscious and they'll feed on my body when I'm dead." She began to cry again.

She sat there until the thunder began to move east and the rain stopped. She was hungry now. She took off her poncho and opened her pack. Her lunch was a boiled egg, a fish sandwich and some celery. There was also the bag of potato chips, the bottle of water, the bottle of soda and the Twinkies. Looking at the bottle of soda, Trisha was suddenly more thirsty than hungry. She took the top off the bottle. Then she had a thought.

"Don't drink too much," she told herself. "You might be out here for hours yet." She took three big drinks, then put the top back on the bottle.

Next she ate the egg. Then she looked at the Twinkies. She opened the package and ate one of them. Next she had a drink of the water. After that, she quickly put the rest of the food and drink back into her pack.

And then Trisha found her Walkman[18]!

She took it carefully out of the pack, put the headphones over her ears, and pushed the switch from TAPE to RADIO. At first she heard nothing, but after a moment or two she found WCAS, the little radio station at Castle Rock. It was good to hear human voices! She sat quietly and listened to the music.

And she listened to the phone calls from people who wanted to sell washing machines and cars. At three-thirty there was some local news. But the news didn't include anything about a girl lost in the woods. And after the news, the woman announcer[19] said, "Don't forget that the Boston Red Sox are playing the New York Yankees tonight at seven o'clock. You can hear the game on WCAS. And now back to—"

Trisha switched the radio off. She felt better now, after eating some food and hearing human voices.

She suddenly thought of something which she had read in a book. It was about finding your way out of the woods by using water. What had it said? And then she remembered. You found a stream and you followed it. The stream would lead you out of the woods. Or it would lead you to a bigger stream, which you followed until *that* led you out of the woods, or to a bigger stream again. Water had to lead you out of the woods sometime, because it always went to the sea.

Trisha put her pack on—over her poncho this time—and she started walking through the woods again. The cliff edge and the valley were on her right. And after a time, she heard the sound of running water.

The sound came from a small stream that ran out of the trees and went down the side of the cliff to the valley. And here, the valley was only twenty feet below her and the cliff was not so steep. The ground on either side of the stream was loose, wet rock, but there were bushes there too.

"I'll follow the stream down into the valley," Trisha thought. "If I start to fall, I can grab one of those bushes."

She went down the cliff in little jumps on the right side of the stream. But halfway down, a wasp[20] flew into her face and stung her near her left eye.

"Aaagh!" Trisha screamed. She hit the insect, but as she did this her foot slipped on a wet rock and she fell. Her shoulder hit some of the loose rocks and she began to slide down over them. She grabbed a bush, but it came out of the ground. Then she was sliding on her back, waving her arms and screaming with pain. As she slid, sharp pieces of rock cut into her shoulders.

"Oh, please help me!" she screamed.

4

The Red Sox and the Yankees

Trisha stopped sliding when she hit a dead tree. A moment later, she was stung by another wasp—twice! Trisha screamed and waved her arms. Then there were wasps all around her. They came flying out of a hole in the dead tree. Another wasp stung her neck, and another stung one of her arms.

She jumped up and ran towards the stream, running through and around bushes. When she reached the stream, she looked over her shoulder. The wasps were gone. But already her left eye was swollen as a result of the wasp sting. Her eye was nearly closed. The sharp pieces of rock had cut into her back, and there was blood on her left arm and on the left side of her face.

She sat down beside the little stream, took off her pack and her poncho, and cried. She cried until she was too tired to cry any more. Then she had a thought. Her Walkman!

Had it gotten broken in her fall?

Trisha's fingers were shaking as she opened her pack. The bag of potato chips was broken, but the two bottles—one with water, one with soda—were OK. And the Walkman was OK too!

It looks OK, but maybe it's broken inside. It was the voice inside her head whispering to her.

Trisha put the headphones on, put her finger on the switch, and closed her eyes. "Please, God," she said aloud. "Please let it be OK." She pushed the switch to RADIO.

"Some news has just come in," the woman announcer said. "A nine-year-old girl, Patricia McFarland, is lost in the woods west of TR-90 and the town of Motton. Patricia was walking with her mother and brother on the Appalachian Trail when she disappeared."

Trisha listened for the next ten minutes, long after the news report, and after WCAS started playing music again. She was lost in the woods. It was on the radio! Now people would start looking for her. There were people who kept helicopters ready to fly and dogs ready to search.

At last she switched off her Walkman and put it back into her pack. She sat eating potato chips and waving bugs away from her face. She was about to put her poncho back on when she noticed the mud on the sides of the stream. She stopped and put a finger into the soft wet mud.

"Shall I try it?" she thought. "It can't hurt me."

Carefully, Trisha put mud on each of the wasp stings. It was wonderfully cool and it helped to soothe[21] the pain. Then she wiped her hands on her jeans, and put on her poncho and her pack.

She began walking beside the stream again. Five minutes

later she was among the trees at the bottom of the valley.

———

Trisha followed the stream for the next four hours. She heard nothing but the songs of birds and the buzzing sounds of bugs. It started to rain again. For a while, it rained hard enough to make her wet all over, but at least there was no thunder or lightning. She tried to imagine hundreds of people searching for her. In her head, she saw a picture of buses driving into parking lots. The parking lots were all along the part of the Appalachian Trail which ran through western Maine. All the buses had signs with the words SEARCH PARTY[22] in their front windows. Men, some with dogs, came out from the buses with walkie-talkies[23]. A few men had bull horns[24].

"I'll hear someone's voice through a bull horn before I see them," Trisha thought. "They'll be shouting, 'Patricia McFarland, where are you? If you can hear me, come to the sound of my voice!' I'm sure that I'll hear someone soon!"

But as the afternoon went by and the shadows in the woods became darker, nobody came for her. Soon, Trisha could only hear the sound of the stream and the sound of her own breathing.

"I can't stay out here all night," she said to herself. "No one can expect me to stay out here all night!" Trisha was afraid of the dark, even when she was at home in her room. "I'll die of fear if I have to stay all night in these woods."

Suddenly, Trisha wanted to run. She had been following this stream for miles now and she wanted to run away from it. She wanted to run and find people before it got dark. She pushed through some trees which were very close together, and came out in a little open place—a clearing. There were bushes and trees on all sides of it, but there was also part of a fallen tree to sit on.

Trisha went to the tree and sat down. She closed her eyes and tried to think. What was the best thing to do? She tried to pray. Her parents didn't attend church and she didn't know the right words to say. And who would she say them to, anyway? To God? Who was God?

A month before, Trisha had asked her father if *he* believed in God.

"God?" Larry McFarland said. "I'm not sure about God, but—" He stopped and he thought for several minutes while Trish waited quietly. They were sitting behind Dad's house in Malden, eating ice-cream. Pete was out with his friends. At last her father said, "I'll tell you what I believe in. I believe in the Sub-audible."

"You believe in *what?*" Trisha asked in surprise.

"In the Sub-audible," her father replied. "Do you remember our house on Fore Street?"

"Yes, of course I remember it."

"It had lots of noises," he said. "All houses have noises. The motor of the refrigerator starts and stops. The wooden floors make creaking sounds. The traffic goes by outside. We hear all those things all the time, so most of the time we don't *notice* them. They become—" He waited.

"Sub-audible," Trisha said, completing his sentence.

"That's right!" he continued. "Sub-audible. I don't believe in a God who thinks. I don't believe there's a God who knows what each of us is doing all the time. But I believe that there is *something* which is bigger than us. It's the thing that stops teenagers from crashing their cars. It's the thing that stops planes from crashing even when their control systems break down—not all planes, just most of them. It's the thing that keeps us from dying in our sleep. Yes, there must be Something.`

"And that Something is the Sub-audible," she said.

"Yes." Trisha's dad smiled. "I also believe that Tom Gordon can win forty games for the Red Sox this year. I believe that he's the best closer[25] in the major leagues, and he could be pitching in the World Series in October. Is that enough belief for you?"

"Yes, that's enough!" she replied, laughing.

But now, Trisha was sitting on the fallen tree, as the sky started to grow darker. And she found that it *wasn't* enough.

"I can't pray to the Sub-audible," she thought. "I just can't do that." And she couldn't pray to Tom Gordon—that would be stupid. But perhaps she could listen to the description of him pitching against the Yankees on WCAS.

Trisha opened her backpack and carefully took out the Walkman. She put on the headphones, then pushed the switch, and suddenly her head was full of sound. The radio station was broadcasting the baseball game at Fenway Park. She heard the voices of Joe Castiglione and Jerry Trupiano, the two commentators[26].

"—and at the end of two and a half innings," Jerry was saying, "this is the score. It's still Yankees two, Boston Red Sox nothing."

Trisha thought about the time. She didn't have a watch with her. But two and a half innings of the game had been played already, so it had to be eight o'clock. She'd been on her own for ten hours now! Trisha waved away the bugs and opened her pack again. She sat listening to the game and slowly ate half of her sandwich. She put the other half back in the pack, then ate the rest of the Twinkies. She had three big drinks of soda, and ate the last potato chips as the Red Sox and the Yankees played through the rest of the third and the fourth innings.

By the middle of the fifth inning the score was Yankees four, and the Red Sox one. Trisha knew that she ought to switch off the radio before she used up the power in the batteries. But she didn't want to lose the sound of people. She didn't want to hear the buzzing of the mosquitoes, the rain falling from the bushes—and any other sounds there might be.

It was the other sounds she was most afraid of—other sounds in the dark. And it was dark now.

Soon, the Red Sox were leading five to four! And Tom Gordon came in to pitch!

Trisha fell off the tree and onto the ground. "Tom must keep the one-run lead and beat the Yankees!" she thought. It was the most important thing in the world.

"Come on, Tom," she whispered. "You can do it!"

———

In a hotel room in the town of Castle View, Trisha's mother was sick with worry. Larry McFarland, her ex-husband, was on a plane, flying from Boston to Portland. He was coming to be with her and their son. Outside the Castle View County police building, search parties were gathering after their first search in the woods. They had returned for some rest. More than thirty other men, some with dogs, were continuing to look for Trisha.

"She must still be in the Motton or TR-90 areas," the men outside the police building said to each other. "She's only a little girl. She probably isn't far from where she was last seen."

In fact, Trisha was almost nine miles west of the area they'd been searching. The men would have been shocked if they'd known that.

—————

"Come on, Tom," Trisha whispered as she listened to her Walkman. "Come on!"

"If we win—if Tom gets the save," she thought, "then *I'll* be saved."

The thought had come suddenly into her head. It was stupid, of course. But as the woods got darker and darker, it seemed right to Trisha. If Tom Gordon got the save, she would get the save too.

On the radio, the crowd at Fenway Park was cheering. Trisha imagined them moving forward in their seats. "Come on, Tom, come on," she whispered again.

Gordon was pitching to Tino Martinez. He threw his curveball[27].

"This is great!" Joe Castiglione shouted. "The Red Sox have just a one-run lead. Tom Gordon is on the mound, and now Darryl Strawberry is coming to the plate. And Darryl is always a dangerous player."

"Aaagh! Why did you have to say that?" Trisha whispered to the radio. "Saying it makes him more dangerous!"

"Gordon throws—and Strawberry misses," said Jerry Trupiano, the commentator. "Strike one!"

"Come on Tom, oh, come on!" Trisha said excitedly.

"Gordon's ready again," Joe said. "He throws—Strawberry swings and it's a long hit. But the ball isn't going where Strawberry wanted it to go. It's a foul!"

Trisha was so excited she had forgotten about being lost.

"Gordon throws again. The ball is on the ground. But

"If we win—if Tom gets the save, then I'll be saved."

Veritek stopped it with his body and that has saved a run," Joe said. "Strawberry is ready again. Gordon throws! The crowd is standing now—all thirty thousand people."

Trisha could see them inside her head.

"Gordon pitches—and it's strike three! Gordon threw a curveball and Strawberry didn't know what to do! The Red Sox win five to four over the Yankees and Tom Gordon gets his eighteenth save!"

Trisha was crying now. But she was crying because she was happy. She was lost, but someone would find her soon. Tom Gordon had got the save and so would she!

"And Gordon is doing what he always does after a save!" Jerry said.

Trisha switched off her Walkman and put it back into her pack. She didn't need to listen any more. She *knew* what Tom Gordon always did after a save. He always pointed at the sky with the first finger of his right hand.

Now the voices from the radio were gone Trisha suddenly remembered where she was. She was alone in the woods, in the dark. She wanted her mother. And she wanted her father—she wanted him even more than her mother. Dad would be able to get her out of here. He would carry her when she was tired. He was big and strong. And she was so small and afraid!

Soon, Trisha fell asleep with her head on her arm. A light wind blew through the trees for a while and then everything went silent. But later there was a sound of something moving through the trees. Then there was the rough sound of noisy breathing. The sound moved closer and closer to the place where Trisha was sleeping.

5

The Thing in the Woods

"Get off me! Get off me!" Trisha screamed. She had woken to find bugs and mosquitoes crawling over her and flying around her face. She waved her hands in front of her eyes. "Go away!" she screamed.

She had been bitten by bugs while she slept. Her body was itching all over. When she tried to stand up, she found that her left arm and left leg were numb[28] and she had to crawl across to the stream. The moon was bright in the night sky. When she looked up at it, she felt more alone than ever.

Trisha bent over the stream and splashed some water onto her face. In the bright moonlight, she could see her reflection in the stream. The wasp-sting under her left eye had swollen some more, and the rest of her face was covered with mosquito bites. She splashed water onto her neck and arms, and it was wonderfully cool on her hot skin. Then she put mud on her face and neck, and on her arms and hands.

Her arm and leg were OK now, but her neck hurt when she moved it to the right or left. Trisha put a hand on her neck and rubbed it carefully. Maybe the searchers would take her to hospital in a helicopter when they found her, and—

There won't be any helicopter ride for you, Trisha. It was the cold, scary voice in her head again. *They're never going to find you. You'll die of hunger out here in the woods. The animals will eat your body. And one day, a hunter will find your bones.*

Trisha started to cry again. She had heard stories like this on the TV news. In her mind, she could see the hunter, a man in a red jacket and an orange cap. "He sees something

33

white and thinks that it's only a stone," she told herself. "But when he gets nearer, he sees that the stone has eye-holes!"

"Stop it," she whispered, walking back to the fallen tree.

But the cold voice in her head had more to say. *Maybe you won't die of hunger. Maybe the Thing out there will kill you and eat you.*

Trisha stopped by the fallen tree and looked around nervously. The moonlight on the trees made black shadows on the ground. When the wind blew through the trees, the shadows moved and changed in a frightening way.

Far away, a bird made a noise. Nearer, a tree branch broke with a SNAP!

"What was that?" Trisha thought, turning towards the sound.

"Nothing, it was nothing," she told herself.

It isn't nothing, it's the Thing, Trisha. The cold voice was in her head again. *It's coming for you.*

"There *is* no Thing," Trisha said aloud. "There is no Thing!"

The moonlight had changed the shapes of the trees. It had turned them into bone faces with black eyes. And the sound of two branches rubbing together became the sound of a monster. Trisha turned quickly, trying to look everywhere at once.

It's a special Thing, Trisha—the Thing that waits for the lost ones. It waits until they're really scared, because fear makes them taste better. You'll see it soon. It will come out of the trees any minute now. And when you see its face, you'll go crazy. You'll laugh, and laugh, and laugh—

"Stop it, there is nothing in the woods! Stop it!" She

whispered this very fast. "Sounds are just sounds. Shadows are just shadows. There is no *Thing* in the woods."

There is!

And there was.

Now, stopping her thoughts and holding her breath, Trisha listened. She knew that there was a Thing. Inside her, at that moment, there were no voices, only a part of her that she didn't understand. That part didn't see and it couldn't think, but it could feel. And now it *felt* something in the woods.

"Hello?" she called to the moonlight-and-bone faces of the trees. "Hello, is someone there?"

———

In the Castle View hotel room, Larry McFarland sat on one of the beds with his arm round his ex-wife's shoulders. Her body was shaking.

"It's all right," he said. "It was only a bad dream."

"No!" she said. "Trisha is in danger—I feel it. She's in terrible danger." And she began to cry wildly.

———

In the woods, Trisha was not crying. She was too scared to cry at that moment. Something was watching her. *Something.*

"Hello?" she called again. There was no answer. But it was there, and it was moving somewhere behind the trees, moving from left to right. She heard the sound of a branch breaking. "Don't hurt me," Trisha said to it, and now she did start to cry. "Whatever you are, please don't hurt me. I won't try to hurt *you*. But please don't hurt me. I'm just a kid."

Still crying, she crawled under the wide trunk of the fallen tree. She pulled her backpack after her.

Was the thing high up in the trees? Was it moving

"Trisha is in danger—I feel it. She's in terrible danger."

through the branches? Maybe it was something with wings. She looked out at the trees, but she saw only branches against the night sky. There was no *Thing* among them. And now the woods were silent. No birds called, no bugs buzzed in the grass.

But the Thing was very close, whatever it was. Trisha knew that. And it was making a decision. Either it would come and kill her or it would move away. Trisha lay holding her pack against her body and tried not to breathe. After a long time, another branch broke—SNAP! But this one was farther from her tree. Whatever the Thing was, it was moving away from her. She closed her eyes.

"I wish that I was dead," she whispered to herself. "It's better to be dead than to be so scared. It's better to be dead than to be lost."

Then she heard the sound of another branch breaking, still farther away. Yes, the Thing was going, but it knew that she was here now. It knew that she was here in its woods. It would come back.

"I'll never get to sleep again," Trisha thought. "Never."

Then she thought of her mother. Her mother always told Trisha to imagine something nice when she couldn't go to sleep. She could try that. But what should she imagine? Suddenly, she knew the answer. She imagined that Tom Gordon was with her. In her mind, Tom was standing by the stream.

"What was that in the woods?" she asked him.

"I don't know, Trisha," Tom replied.

"What's the secret?" she asked, sleepily. "The secret of closing?"

"You have to—"

But Trisha was asleep now.

———

In the Castle View hotel her parents were also asleep. In the same room. In the same bed. In the room next to them, Pete McFarland was also asleep. Pete was having a bad dream. In the dream, he and his mother were walking along the trail, arguing. He turned and looked back down the trail—and Trisha wasn't there. There was only the empty path.

"No!" Pete shouted in his sleep, shaking his head from side to side. "No!"

6

Fiddlehead Island

When Trisha woke up the next morning, her neck hurt and it was difficult to turn her head. But the sun was shining and she felt more cheerful. She remembered waking in the night. She remembered putting more mud on her stings and bites. She remembered going to sleep while Tom Gordon was with her. She also remembered being very frightened of something in the woods.

"But there was nothing watching me really," she told herself. "It was being alone in the dark that frightened me."

She crawled out from under the fallen tree and went to the stream. She washed the mud from her face and hands. Immediately there were bugs and mosquitoes buzzing around her head. She put some more mud on her face. Next she washed her hands in the stream again, then she ate the rest of her sandwich and half of the celery. Now all she had left was a little celery, half a bottle of soda and half a bottle of water.

"That's OK, because there are going to be lots of search parties looking for me," she told herself. She put the rest of the celery back into her pack, and pushed her poncho in after it.

"By noon, I'll be having a good hot meal somewhere," she said aloud.

After putting her things in her pack, Trisha put more mud on her hands and then moved her head and neck around. She listened for searchers' voices. She listened for the sound of a helicopter. But there was nothing to hear.

"It's all right. There's plenty of time," she told herself. "It's June. These are the longest days of the year. I'll follow the stream. And if the search parties don't find me soon, the stream will take me to people."

But as the morning went by, the stream only took her to woods, and more woods. And again she was sure that she was being watched. When she stopped to rest, she heard sounds nearby. She turned around very slowly and she saw nothing. But the woods were silent again, except for the noise of buzzing mosquitoes.

"Who's there?" she called.

There was no answer of course, and Trisha moved on. The stream was getting narrower. Was it going to disappear into a hole in the ground? It ran into some bushes. Trisha pushed through the bushes to stay beside the stream. She was afraid of losing it. Without it, she would just be a kid lost in the woods, with no plan.

She walked with her head down, looking at the ground.

She didn't notice that many of the trees here were dead. But neither did she notice that the ground under her feet was getting softer.

Then the stream began to get wider again. It was about noon now. For about fifteen minutes Trisha hoped that the stream wasn't going to disappear, after all. But the stream was not as deep here. And ten minutes later, one of her shoes sank deep into the soft ground. Trisha pulled her foot out with a little cry. Her shoe had nearly come off her foot. She pushed the shoe back on and looked around.

She saw that she had come to a part of the woods where there had once been a fire. In front of her were dead, burned trees, and the ground under them was soft and wet.

It was a swamp[29]. And Trisha's stream disappeared into the soft wet ground!

"What do I do now?" she asked aloud. "Will somebody please tell me what to do?" But of course nobody answered. Nobody could hear her.

There were lots of places to sit and think about it. There were dead, fallen trees everywhere. She sat on one.

"Well, I have a choice," Trisha thought. "I can stay here and hope that somebody comes to rescue me. Or I can keep moving and try to meet a search party. There's nothing to eat here, and it smells of mud and dead trees. If I stay here and no search party comes, I'll have to sleep here tonight."

That was a terrible thought.

She looked through the dead trees and their gray branches. Was that something green she could see beyond them? Maybe it was a hill. And maybe there were more checkerberry bushes there? Trisha realized that she was hungry again.

She stood up and moved forward a few steps. Then she

stopped. She watched water come up from the ground and cover the front of her shoe. She moved back and sat down again.

"Go or stay? Stay or go?" she asked herself. She thought about the berries. She closed her eyes. In her head, she saw herself picking bright red berries on the side of a pleasant green hill. She saw herself filling her pack with berries, then reaching the top of the hill. She would look down and see—

"A road. Yes, I'll see a road with fences on each side. And horses in a field. And—"

This was crazy! Or was it? Maybe she was sitting only half an hour's walk from safety. And she would never find out if she was afraid of getting her feet wet!

"OK," she said aloud, standing up again.

She started walking slowly and carefully over the wet ground and around the dead trees. After half an hour, it was too late to go back. She had to go on. Suddenly her foot went deep into the ground. She screamed and fell forward into the long grass. She pulled her foot out of the ground. It came out with a loud sound—PLOP! But her shoe stayed down under the ground.

"No!" she shouted. "You can't have it! It's mine!"

She pushed her hand down into the muddy, watery hole, and after a second she pulled out her shoe. It was black with mud. Trisha began to cry. Then she started to laugh. For a minute or two she sat on the grass with the rescued shoe, laughing and crying, with bugs flying around her head. Then she stopped and cleaned the shoe with some grass.

She stood up with the shoe in her hand and looked ahead. Now she could see the green place which she had thought was a hill. It wasn't a hill. It was just some small hummocks[30]

41

of grass in the swamp.

"Well, you can go back," she told herself. "You know the way."

Did she know the way? Maybe. Maybe not. She looked at the dead trees and grass hummocks in front of her. The swamp had to end somewhere. Maybe the best plan was to go on.

"You're crazy to even think about it," she told herself.

But she wanted to get out of this place, out of this horrible swamp. And then she wanted to get out of the woods. She wanted to get back to a place where there were people. She wanted people and shopping malls and police officers who helped you when you lost your way.

Trisha took off her other shoe. She tied the shoes together by their laces, and hung them around her neck. Then she pushed the legs of her jeans up to her knees and started moving again. She jumped from one hummock of grass to the next. An hour went by. Then two hours. And then the hummocks were too far apart to jump between.

She stepped into the swamp. Immediately, the water came almost up to her knees and her feet were sinking into something cold and horrible.

Walking was difficult. She had to pull each foot out of the mud. At last she reached the next grassy hummock and pulled herself up on to it. She took off her black, muddy socks and laughed at her white feet. She laughed and laughed, like a crazy person. Then she squeezed the mud and water from her socks and put them back on.

She tried to walk in a straight line through the swamp. She was hungry, but she tried not to think about that. Once she stopped to drink from her water bottle, and at four o'clock she drank the rest of her soda. As she drank, her foot hit a dead branch and she fell over into the swamp. She got a mouthful of dirty water before she pushed herself up again.

"I'm OK," she said quickly. "I'm OK. I'm fine."

She had fallen on her front, so her backpack was still dry. This was important because her Walkman was inside it.

Wet and dirty, Trisha walked on, moving towards the next dead tree. Soon, she began talking to Tom Gordon again. At first this felt strange. But as the long hours of the afternoon went by, she often talked to him. She told him that she was OK and that she would soon be out of this place. She was telling him that she hoped the Red Sox would win that evening's game, when she stopped suddenly.

"Do you hear something?" she asked him.

Trisha *had* heard something. It was the sound of a helicopter. It was far away, but it was a helicopter, she was sure of that. She turned around in a circle, looking up at the sky. But she couldn't see the helicopter. And a moment later, she couldn't hear it any more.

"Well, they're looking for me," she told Tom Gordon.

She hit a mosquito on her neck and started moving again.

Ten minutes later, she was standing on a fallen tree branch and looking ahead. Beyond the fallen trees, the swamp opened up into a wide flat pond. Across the center of the pond were more little hummocks. But most of these were not grass hummocks. They were brown and they were made from broken tree branches and half-eaten bits of wood. Sitting on top of several of the hummocks were six or seven fat brown animals.

Suddenly, Trisha forgot about being in the swamp, about

43

Sitting on top of several of the hummocks were six or seven fat brown animals.

being wet, muddy and tired. And she forgot about being lost.

"Tom!" she whispered. "Those are beavers[31]! They're beavers sitting on beaver-houses!"

She stared at the animals, smiling. Were they watching her? Yes! One beaver was bigger than the others, and was staring at her with his black eyes. He was beautiful!

At last, Trisha started moving again. Immediately, the big beaver slipped into the water and made a slapping sound with his tail. A moment later all the beavers were jumping into the water.

"Tom, look!" Trisha said, laughing. "There they go!"

Then they were gone, and Trisha moved towards a large, grassy hummock with dark green plants growing on it. She moved carefully. Beavers had sharp teeth and she did not want to meet one that was swimming under the water.

As she got nearer to the hummock, she began to get excited. She knew what the plants were. They were fiddlehead ferns. Fiddleheads were good to eat! And there were lots of them. This wasn't just a hummock, it was Fiddlehead Island!

But there were thousands of bugs there, too. Why?

Something wasn't right. Now Trisha could see dark red marks on the green ferns. There was something dead or hurt up there. She moved to the left instead of going straight ahead. Halfway along the side of Fiddlehead Island she stopped to look.

"Look, Tom," she said. "Oh, that's bad!"

It was the head of a small deer—just the head. It was near the water's edge. There were bugs and flies in its eyes and on its neck, and blood on the fiddlehead ferns around it.

"Well, I won't be eating any ferns," Trisha told herself.

She pushed on through the swamp, not looking back.

What had killed the deer? It couldn't have been a beaver.

It was the Thing. The cold voice was speaking in her head again. *It was the Thing which is watching you now.*

"Nothing's watching me," she said aloud. "That's stupid, isn't it, Tom?"

But Tom didn't answer. Tom couldn't answer. Tom was probably at Fenway Park now, getting ready for the evening's baseball game. She was alone.

But you're not alone. You're not alone at all.

Trisha was terribly afraid that the cold voice was right. That feeling of being watched had returned. It was stronger than ever.

A few minutes later, she came to a tree and she saw six or seven deep cuts on it.

"Oh, God," she said. "Those are claw-marks."

Yes. It's ahead of you, Trisha. It's ahead of you and waiting for you with its sharp claws.

She could see more hummocks, and something like another green hill. And she moved forward again because it was too far to go back. It was too far even if something was waiting to kill her.

Now the water wasn't as deep as it had been half a mile back. There were more fiddleheads growing on two of the hummocks. She picked some and ate them quickly. They were sweet, but very good. But when she reached towards the last few fiddleheads on the second hummock, her hand stopped. She heard the buzzing of the flies again, much louder now. Trisha wanted to move away quickly from the hummock, but here the swamp was full of dead branches and bushes.

She climbed over a fallen tree and saw the deep cut marks on its side. But it wasn't a *fallen* tree. It hadn't fallen.

Something had pushed it over. Some *thing*. The buzzing got louder.

The rest of the deer's body was lying amongst the fiddle-heads. It was in two pieces, with thousands of flies on its open stomach. Trisha put the back of her right hand over her mouth and hurried on, trying not to be sick. She didn't stop until she couldn't hear the buzzing any more.

7

Something Bad in the Water

Trisha took off her socks and then put her shoes on again. She put the socks into her pack and looked up at the sky. She could hear the sound of helicopters. These were much nearer than the first one had been. She jumped up and looked around. And away in the east were two black shapes against the blue sky.

It was stupid to wave because they were too far away to see her. But she waved and she shouted until her throat hurt.

"Look, Tom," she said at last. "They're trying to find me."

But then the helicopters disappeared behind the trees in the distance. Trisha stood still until she couldn't hear them any more, then she walked on.

She was still hungry and she was thirsty now. Her throat was dry.

"I'm not going to die of thirst in the woods, am I, Tom?" she asked.

But the real Tom Gordon was busy with the game now.

Trisha walked on. The trees were taller here, and the orange-red light of the last of the day's sun came through them. It was beautiful, but Trisha's head hurt and she was too thirsty to enjoy the sight. And when she heard the sound of running water, she thought that she was dreaming.

But she turned towards it, at first walking quickly and then running. Ten minutes later, she came to the edge of a ravine. She looked down. Twenty feet below was a stream, deep and fast-moving. She walked along the edge of the ravine for five minutes and then came to a narrow channel which led down to the stream. The floor of the channel was covered with dead leaves.

Trisha sat down at the top and started to slide down the leafy channel. Down, down she went, sitting at first and then lying back with her hands behind her head. A rock hit her side and another hit her hands. And then she was at the bottom, with her feet in ice-cold water. She pulled them out, turned around onto her front, and started drinking.

The water tasted wonderful! Trisha had never drunk anything as good as this!

At last she stopped drinking and stood up. The channel was too steep and too slippery to climb up again. After thinking for a moment or two, Trisha picked up four large stones, one at a time, and dropped them into the stream. She used these to walk across the deep stream to the other side.

She followed the stream down a hill, and when it came to an open place among the trees, Trisha decided to stop for the night. There were a lot of bugs, and she waved away the mosquitoes that were flying around her face. She bent over

48

Down, down she went.

the stream to get some mud, but there was no mud, only rocks. So she made some mud, using water from the stream and earth from the ground. She put it on her face and arms.

There were no fallen trees to sleep under, but Trisha saw some dead branches on the ground. She carried some of these to one of the tall trees and stood them against its trunk. This made a little shelter that she could crawl into.

As she put the last two branches against the tree, she felt a sharp pain in her stomach.

It was the water. She heard the cold voice in her head again. *There was something bad in the water. You'll probably be dead by the morning.*

"OK, then I'll be dead," Trisha said angrily. "I *had* to drink the water because I was so thirsty."

After a while, the pain went away, but her stomach didn't feel quite right. She tried not to think about it and took off her backpack. She took out her Walkman, put the headphones over her ears and switched the radio on.

"OK," Joe Castiglione was saying. His voice seemed to come from far away. "We're ready for the fourth inning."

Suddenly Trisha rolled away from her shelter and got on to her knees. She crawled to another tree which was nearby. She put one hand on the tree and the other hand on her stomach. A second later, she was terribly sick. She stayed with her head down for a moment or two, and then she was sick again.

After a minute, she pushed herself away from the tree. But now the sharp pain was lower down inside her.

"Oh, no!" she cried. "I need the bathroom!"

But there was no bathroom, of course.

She quickly pulled off her jeans and her underwear.

Everything from inside her came out as hot, wet liquid.

After it was finished, she went to the stream and washed the backs of her legs. She felt weak and her body was shaking.

"It was the water, Tom," she said quietly. "But I *had* to drink it."

She put her clothes on again and crawled into her shelter. She lay listening to the Red Sox game for some time, but she was very thirsty again. Very, very thirsty. So she went to the stream and drank more water. It was cold and wonderful. "But I probably *will* be dead by morning," she thought.

The Red Sox lost the game and Tom Gordon didn't get to pitch. Trisha switched off the Walkman and began to cry. She was still crying when she fell asleep.

———

At about that time, at the Maine State Police building in Castle View, a short phone call was received.

"The girl you're looking for was taken off the trail by Francis Raymond Mazzerole," the caller said. "He's thirty-six years old, he wears glasses and has short blond hair. OK?"

The police officer who took the call started to ask a question.

"Sir, can I ask you to—"

"Shut up and listen!" the caller said quickly. "Mazzerole is driving a blue Ford car. He must be in Connecticut by now. He's bad. Look at his police record[32] and you'll see. He'll kill her in a few days. He's done it before."

"Sir, I need to know—" the police officer began.

"I hope you kill him," said the caller and hung up[33].

———

At two o'clock the next morning, Trisha woke up with another terrible pain in her stomach. She knocked down

51

her shelter trying to get out of it quickly. Outside, she pulled down her jeans.

Later, she went across to the other tree. Trisha's Sick Tree, she called it now. Her skin was hot, but her body was shaking.

"I can't be sick any more," she whispered. "Please God, don't make me be sick any more, or it will kill me."

It was then that she saw Tom Gordon for the first time. He was standing in the woods about fifty feet away. He was wearing his baseball glove, and his right hand was behind his back. Trisha knew that there was a baseball in it.

"Tom," she whispered. "You didn't get a chance in the game tonight, did you?"

Tom did not answer. It was time to close. He stood quietly in the moonlight. Waiting. Waiting until the right moment—the special moment—to throw. To close.

"Could I do that?" Trisha asked herself. "Could I stand quietly, until the shaking stops?" She tried.

It didn't happen suddenly, but it did happen. She made herself quiet inside. She was waiting—waiting for the right moment to throw the ball.

The shaking stopped. The pain in her stomach went away.

Then the moon went behind a cloud. Tom Gordon was gone. Of course, he had never really been there at all, Trisha knew that, but—

"He looked real that time," she said. "He looked so real!"

She made her shelter again and crawled into it. Five minutes later, she was asleep. As she slept, something came and watched her. It watched for a long time. When the sky began to get lighter, it went away. But it didn't go far.

8

The Three Robes

When Trisha woke up, the birds were singing and the light was strong and bright. Was it the middle of the morning?

She was very hungry. Her stomach was hurting with hunger. She crawled out of her shelter and went across to the stream. She got down on her knees and drank from it. The water would probably make her sick again, but she had to drink it.

And she had to have some more food. She had finished the food in her backpack.

She stood up and started walking down the hill, beside the stream. After a hundred steps, the cold voice spoke inside her head. *You forgot your pack. Ha, ha!*

The voice was right. Trisha turned round and went back up the hill. She was weak and tired, and she had to stop twice. She filled her water bottle, put it and her poncho into her pack, and started walking down the hill again. She walked slowly. Her head hurt and her eyes hurt when she looked at anything. All the colors looked too bright.

She imagined that Tom Gordon was walking beside her. After a minute, she knew that Tom *was* walking beside her. He was as real in the light of day as he had been in the moonlight.

About the middle of the day, Trisha fell over a rock into some bushes. But when she tried to get up again, she couldn't. Her legs were too weak. She lay with her eyes closed.

"I'm going to die, Tom, aren't I?" she asked.

There was no answer. She opened her eyes and looked around. Tom was gone.

Trisha crawled slowly to the stream and had a drink. The water wasn't hurting her stomach any more. Maybe her stomach was too empty for her to be sick. She sat up and looked along the stream. The direction was northwest, Trisha guessed. There were no sounds of helicopters or dogs.

"I'm going to die in the woods," she said aloud.

At last she got up and started walking again.

———

At the same time, two detectives were talking with Trisha's mother and brother. They were asking questions about the parking lot where they had left their car on Saturday morning. Had Pete or his mother seen a blue Ford there? Had they seen a man with blond hair and glasses?

Trisha's mother began to cry. "Are you saying that my daughter was kidnapped[34]?" she said. "Oh, no! Did somebody take her from behind us while we were arguing?"

And then Pete started to cry, too.

The search was continuing. But now the men and women in the woods were looking for the girl's pack, her poncho, her clothes. They no longer hoped to find the girl herself.

They were looking near the place where the girl was last seen. But Trisha was thirty miles away from there. She was no longer in Maine. At three o'clock that Monday afternoon, she crossed into the state of New Hampshire.

———

It was more than an hour later when Trisha saw the bushes of checkerberries ahead of her. She started to run. When she got to them, she put out her hands. Were the berries real? Or was she dreaming? For a moment she wasn't sure, but then the berries were soft and fat under her fingers! A moment later, she was pushing them quickly into her mouth! Her fingers and hands turned red, and so did her mouth. She ate some of the leaves as well as the berries.

"Mmm! The leaves are good, too!" she thought.

She came out of the bushes—and found herself looking into the dark brown eyes of a deer. Trisha screamed and dropped a handful of berries on the ground. The deer jumped back. There were two young deer behind it, and for a minute the three of them just stood and looked at Trisha. Then they turned and ran away through the trees.

"Goodbye!" Trisha called after them. "Thanks for coming to see me."

And then she saw the nuts on the ground. Hundreds of them! The deer had been eating the nuts, but there were plenty left. They were beechnuts. Trisha picked one up and opened the shell with her fingernails. The nut inside the shell was small, but it tasted good. She took off her backpack and opened it. Then she crawled across the ground, picking up beechnuts and putting them into her pack. Next she went back to the bushes and picked more berries. She put those in her pack too.

When her backpack was nearly full, she went to the stream and sat down under a tree. In the water, she saw a small fish. She smiled, turned her face up to the sun and closed her eyes. She put her hand inside her pack and pulled out some nuts and berries. She laughed, then began to take the shells off ten or twelve of the nuts. She mixed them with the same number of berries, then pushed them all into her mouth. The taste was wonderful!

"You saved my life," she told the nuts and berries in her backpack.

On the other side of the stream, there was a little clearing between the trees. Butterflies flew around in the sunlight in this clearing. There were three of them. Two were white and one was dark brown. Trisha sat and watched the butterflies playing in the afternoon sun, and in that quiet moment she was completely calm and peaceful. She felt so sleepy, so full, so wonderful.

She looked along the stream, and suddenly she noticed that another stream joined it about forty yards away. This second stream came over some rocks in a little waterfall. Good! Now *her* stream would get bigger and bigger, and it would take her to a place where people lived.

She looked back at the little clearing on the other side of the water. Three people were standing there, looking at her. Or she *thought* that they were looking at her. She couldn't see their faces, or their feet. The people were wearing long robes with hoods that hid their faces. Two of the robes were white. The one in the middle was black.

"Who are you?" Trisha called to them. "Will you help me? I'm lost. I've been lost for—"

But how long had she been lost? She couldn't remember. Was it two days or three?

"—I've been lost for a long time. Will you please help me?"

But the people didn't answer. They only stood looking at her.

"Who are you?" Trisha asked. "Tell me who you are!"

The person on the left moved forward. When he lifted his arms to touch his hood, the white sleeves of his robe fell away from his long white fingers. He pushed the hood back so that Trisha could see his face. It was the face of an intelligent

"—I've been lost for a long time. Will you please help me?"

person. It was a lot like the face of Trisha's science teacher at school.

"I come from the God of Tom Gordon," he said. "He can't help you now. There's a lot happening today. He's busy."

He moved back and put his hood up again. After a moment, the other white-robed person moved forward. He pushed back his hood. And his face was her father's face—well, it was *nearly* her father's face.

"Am I dreaming?" Trisha thought.

"Do you come from the Sub-audible?" she asked.

"I *am* the Sub-audible," he replied. "I had to take the shape of someone you know, so that you could see me. But I'm quite weak. I can't do anything for you, Trisha. Sorry."

He moved back, and the black-robed person moved forward. Trisha was suddenly very afraid.

"No!" she said. "No, not you!" She tried to get up, but she couldn't move.

The person lifted his arms to touch his hood. The black sleeves fell away from yellow-white claws. They were the claws that had left the marks on the trees. They were the claws that had pulled off the deer's head, and pulled the animal's body into two pieces.

"No!" Trisha whispered. "No, don't do that, please. I don't want to see your face."

But the claws pushed back the black hood. There was no face there, only the shape of a head. And the shape was made of wasps. They crawled over each other, buzzing. Behind them, Trisha could see an empty eye, a smiling mouth.

"I come from the Thing in the woods," said the buzzing wasp-voice. "I come from the God of the Lost. It has been watching you. It has been waiting for you."

Trisha tried to shout, but only a whisper came from her mouth. "Go away!"

"The world is bad," the wasp-voice said. Its claws moved slowly down the side of its head, pushing through the wasp-skin. Under the skin Trisha saw shining bone. "The skin of the world is made of things which sting," the wasp-voice continued. "You know this now. Under the skin, there is nothing but bone and the God which we all share."

Trisha was crying now. She looked away, down the stream. Then she looked back.

"I don't believe you!" she said. "I don't—"

But the black robed thing with the wasp-voice was gone. All of them were gone. There were only butterflies dancing in the air across the stream. There were eight or nine butterflies now, not three. All of them were different colors. And the light was different. It was a gold-orange color now. Two hours must have had gone by—maybe three. So Trisha must have been asleep.

"It was all a dream," said Trisha. "That's what it always says in story books." But she couldn't remember going to sleep. She got up and went to the stream. There were two big rocks in the water and she used them to cross the water. Suddenly the feeling that somebody was watching her returned. Trisha looked round. There was nothing there—nothing that she could see. But she heard the cold voice in her head again.

It's watching you, waiting for you.

Trisha went to the place where the three robed figures had been standing. But there was nothing to show that they had ever been there. There were no footprints on the ground.

But there was *something* in the woods. What was it?

She walked between young trees that were growing close together. The sun disappeared and the day was suddenly much darker. Here and there, tall birch trees stood like ghosts. And there was something splashed across the trunk of one of them. Trisha looked back nervously over her shoulder. Inside her head a voice was screaming at her. It was telling her to stop, to go back, not to be stupid. But she went on.

Lying below the birch tree were the blood-covered insides of a young deer. Probably one of those that she had seen in the clearing where the beechnuts were. Further into the woods, she saw a tree with more of the deep claw marks on it. They were high up the trunk. Only a very tall man could reach that high. But no *man* had made those marks.

Yes, it has been watching you.

And it was watching her again now. Maybe she *had* dreamed about the three robed people, but she was not dreaming about the marks on the tree or the dead deer. And she wasn't dreaming about those terrible eyes.

Looking quickly on each side of her, Trisha moved back towards the stream. At any moment, she expected to see it in the woods—the God of the Lost. When she got to the stream, she jumped across it, using the rocks. She was sure that the Thing was behind her. When she reached the other side of the stream she turned and looked back. But there was nothing there.

9

"I Want to Go Home!"

Just before it got dark, Trisha came to a rocky place. From there, she could see out over a valley. She looked down into the valley. She was hoping to see lights, but there were none. She looked around her and saw some groups of small rocks, with leaves lying on the ground between them. She dropped her backpack near two of the groups, then broke off some small branches from a tree. She put these on the leaves between the groups of rocks to make a bed. Next she went to the stream for a drink. She had had some more pains in her stomach during the day, but they weren't as bad as earlier.

"Maybe my stomach is getting used to the stream water," she thought.

She went back to her pack and took out her Walkman. She put on the headphones. But before she could find a baseball game to listen to, she heard her own name!

"—nine-year-old Patricia McFarland, who has been missing since Saturday morning," said the voice on the radio. "The Connecticut police today questioned Francis Raymond Mazzerole of Weymouth, Massachusetts. They questioned him for six hours about the missing girl. Mazzerole has a police record for attacking young children. But he told the detectives that he was in Hartford during the weekend, and there are several people who know that this is true. Next, the police—"

But the voice was getting weaker and weaker, and then it disappeared completely. Trisha switched off the Walkman and took off the headphones.

"They used most of the day talking with this man called Mazzerole," she said. "That was stupid!"

She put the Walkman back into her pack and then lay back on her "bed" and put her poncho over her body. There were a million bright stars in the sky. A million, yes! Suddenly, one of them fell down through the sky. It fell halfway across the sky and then it disappeared. It wasn't a star, of course—not a real star. It was a meteor[35].

There was another, and then another. Trisha sat up, her eyes wide open. Then there was a fourth and a fifth. So Trisha had seen not just one meteor, but a meteor shower. She had never seen anything like it.

"Oh, Tom," she whispered, and her voice was shaking. "Tom, look at this. Do you see it? How beautiful it is!"

She was still watching the meteors when she fell asleep. She dreamed of Tom Gordon, but she woke in the middle of the night. Her body was shaking with cold and she stood up. The wind nearly knocked her down again, but she went to the trees and broke off more branches for her "bed". As she walked back with them, she stopped and slowly turned round in a circle.

"Leave me alone!" she shouted. "Go away!"

For a minute, Trisha heard no sound, only the wind in the trees. And then she heard a grunt. It was a low, soft sound, and it wasn't human. Trisha didn't move. Where had the grunt come from? From this side of the stream? From the other side? From the trees? Yes, from the trees! The Thing was in the trees!

She ran to her "bed" and dropped the branches onto it. Then she crawled under them. The Thing was coming now, moving out of the trees. At last, it was coming for her. The

God of the Lost—the wasp-head. Trisha put her arms over her head and waited for the Thing's claws to cut her into pieces.

She fell asleep like that, with her arms over her head. And when she woke in the early light of Tuesday morning, she saw that something had slept nearby. It had laid between another group of rocks. The leaves between the rocks were flat and pushed into the ground in one place. Something had come after she'd gone to sleep. It had come to lie near her, maybe watching her sleep. Maybe it was thinking, "Shall I kill her now, or shall I leave her for one more day?" And it had decided to leave her.

"It's gone, Tom," she said aloud. "It's gone again."

"Yes," said Tom, "but maybe it will come back."

Trisha sat on a rock and ate berries and beechnuts. Then she went to the stream for a drink. She saw some small fish in the water and decided to try catching one. She put her poncho on one of the flat rocks. Then she found a sharp stone and used it to cut the hood off her poncho. She held the hood up and looked at it. Could she catch a fish in it?

Trisha found two large rocks in the stream and stood on them. She looked down between her legs into the water. There were no fish at the moment, but she held the hood in the water and waited. After a moment she saw three fish coming towards her. They swam between the rocks she was standing on. One of them swam past the hood, but the other two swam straight into it!

"Yes!" screamed Trisha excitedly.

She carefully lifted the hood, full of water, in both hands. When she stepped off the rocks, some of the water came out of the hood, and one of the fish with it. The water splashed

After a moment she saw three fish coming towards her.

on her jeans, and the fish fell back into the water and swam away.

Trisha took the hood across to her poncho. Then she poured the water on to the ground and watched the little fish die. She cut it open with the sharp stone. Something wet—more like water than blood—came out of it. Then she pulled out the fish's stomach. This left a bone, and she tried to pull it out too. She got half of it. Next she took the fish to the stream and washed it.

You can't eat the head, Trisha. Not the eyes, Trisha, not the eyes!

"Shut up," she told the cold voice in her head. And she ate half the fish.

The taste was horrible and also wonderful. She ate the rest of it and then waited to see if she was going to be sick. But she wasn't sick, she was OK. She went back to her pack and put the poncho and the hood into it.

"Did I really do that? Did I really eat an uncooked fish?" she asked herself. "Well, I won't think about it. I don't have to think about it or talk about it. I'll never talk about it at home, if I ever *get* home."

She went down into the valley, where her stream ran between the trees. She imagined that Tom Gordon was walking with her again. Tom wanted to know all about her. He wanted to know about her favorite classes at school and about her friend, Pepsi.

Trisha stopped suddenly. She stopped moving and she stopped talking. She stared at the stream for nearly a minute, waving the bugs away from her face.

"No," Trisha said quietly. "No, not again."

The water in the stream was not as deep as it had been,

65

and it was moving much more slowly.

"If the stream runs into another swamp, I'll kill myself, Tom," she said.

———

An hour later, there was no stream to follow. The water had spread over a large area of land, making a marsh[36]. The marsh didn't look as dangerous as the swamp. But it was at least a mile across, from where Trisha was standing to the next group of trees.

Trisha sat down and started to say something to Tom Gordon. Then she decided that it was stupid to imagine things when she was going to die. She put her face in her hands and began to cry.

"I want my mother!" she shouted. "I want my brother. I want to go home!"

Then she got angry. She started kicking her legs up and down until one of her shoes flew off. "I want my MOTHER! I want my BROTHER! I want to get out of here, DO YOU HEAR ME? Why don't you find me, you stupid people?" she screamed. "I . . . WANT . . . TO . . . GO . . . HOME!"

She lay on her back looking up at the sky. Her stomach hurt and her throat hurt from screaming, but she felt better. She put an arm over her face and, after a few minutes, she fell asleep.

When she woke up, it was afternoon. Her head felt hot. "You shouldn't have slept in the heat of the sun," she told herself. "That was stupid." She put her shoe back on and then she ate some berries and drank some stream water from her bottle. There were fiddlehead ferns growing at the edge of the marsh, and she ate some of them, too.

Trisha stood up and looked across the marsh. She saw the

trees on the far side, standing on a low hill.

"I can't do it," she said. "I can't walk across another wet, muddy field with my shoes around my neck. And why *should* I do it? There's no stream to follow. I won't reach anywhere where there are people."

She turned north and walked along the east side of the marsh.

That was a bad mistake. It was Trisha's worst mistake since leaving the path on the first day. If she had crossed the marsh and climbed up the little hill, she could have looked down at Devlin Pond. This was a place just outside the town of Green Mount, New Hampshire. Devlin Pond was small, but there were cottages at its south end, and a road leading out to Route 52. On a Saturday or Sunday, there were always lots of boats on the pond. But even on that day, there were two men quietly fishing there.

Instead of finding the pond, Trisha turned and began to walk further into the woods. Four hundred miles in front of her was Montreal, in Canada—and there weren't many people between where she was and the St. Lawrence River!

10

The Late Innings

For Trisha, a strange thing happened during the four days that followed. Soon, the difference between "real" and "imaginary" began to disappear. By Saturday it didn't seem to matter any more. Trisha didn't know that it was Saturday, of course. She didn't know what day of the week it was. But by then, Tom Gordon was with her all the time, and he was not "imaginary", but "real". Her friend Pepsi also walked with her some of the time, and they sang songs together. Then Pepsi walked behind a tree and didn't reappear. Trisha looked behind the tree and saw that Pepsi wasn't hiding there. Then she understood. Pepsi had never been there at all. When she understood that, Trisha sat down and cried.

Later, while she was crossing a wide clearing, a large black helicopter appeared over her head. She waved to it and screamed for help, but it flew away and never returned. By then, she had come to an old forest of tall trees. This was on Thursday. The bodies of dead deer hung from these trees. There were thousands of them, all covered with flies. Trisha closed her eyes, and when she opened them the dead deer were gone.

She found a stream and looked into it. She saw a big face at the bottom. The face looked up at her and spoke, but no sound came from its mouth. She walked beside the stream for several hours before it disappeared. Then she passed a great gray tree, shaped like a hand. From inside the tree, a dead voice spoke her name. Several times she heard people calling for her, but when she called back there was never any answer.

But as well as these strange things—things that were like dreams—she remembered finding more checkerberries. She remembered picking them from the bushes and putting them into her backpack. She remembered filling her water bottle from a stream. She remembered falling over a rock onto the ground, her face lying next to the most beautiful flowers she had ever seen.

For many hours she felt sick and hot, and she did not

seem to be in the real world at all. The light from the sun hurt her eyes. She talked and talked—to Tom Gordon, her mother, her brother, her father, Pepsi, and all the teachers at her school.

But later, she remembered best the nights when she sat and listened to the Red Sox games on her Walkman. They won two out of three games in Oakland, with Tom Gordon getting saves in both wins. She was careful with the Walkman batteries. Even when she was sick and her head and stomach hurt, she never went to sleep leaving the Walkman on. Not once. Without it, without the games, she was sure that she would just lie down and die.

When Trisha left the trail and went into the woods she had weighed ninety-seven pounds. When she climbed up a little hill to a clearing seven days later she weighed no more than seventy-eight pounds. Her face was swollen with mosquito bites and her arms were as thin as sticks. She had to pull her jeans up every few minutes because they were too big for her thin body.

Trisha had had good luck with the weather, which had never been very bad. And she had been stronger than she could ever have imagined. But now as she walked through the clearing at the top of the hill, she was almost too weak and too tired to go on.

———

The search parties were still searching, but they were looking for a body now. Everyone thought that she had died. Trisha's parents didn't expect to see their daughter alive again. Pete almost never spoke to anyone now. In his world of electric lights and cars and roads, he thought Trisha was dead.

———

And in her world where sometimes there were dead deer hanging from trees, Trisha was near to death. But she kept moving. The Thing in the woods walked with her, and she knew he—the God of the Lost—was there.

"He'll stay with me now until I die," she said to herself. "And that will happen soon now."

Halfway across a clearing, she began to cough. Her chest hurt when she coughed, and she had to bend over and hold onto the lower part of a broken tree—the stump. Trisha coughed and coughed. When at last she stopped coughing, she looked at the tree stump. She looked at it for a whole minute.

"It's not real," she thought. "I'm not really seeing what I think I'm seeing. It's just another strange dream."

She closed her eyes for twenty seconds and then opened them again.

But she wasn't dreaming. The tree stump wasn't a tree stump. It was a gatepost.

"A gate!" Trisha said. "There's been a gate here."

A gate—that was something made by humans. Something from the wonderful world of electric lights and houses and people. For a few moments, Trisha felt happy.

"This is your last chance, Trisha," Tom Gordon said.

"What do you mean?" she replied. She looked at him.

"It's the late innings now," he said. "Don't make a mistake here, Trisha."

"Tom, you—"

But there was nobody there. Tom was gone. She had not seen him disappear because Tom had never been there at all. She had only imagined him.

"Your last chance." Trisha said to herself. "Late innings.

"This is your last chance, Trisha," Tom Gordon said.

Don't make a mistake."

It was a gatepost, so there had to be a second one. Trisha got down on the ground and crawled in a straight line. One knee forward, then the other—

"Ow!" she yelled in pain, and pulled her hand out of the grass. She looked and saw blood on it, then pushed the grass away to see the stump of the other gatepost. It was broken off about twelve inches out of the ground. The top of it, where it was broken, was as sharp as a knife. A little beyond the stump, fallen in the grass, was the rest of the gatepost.

"Last chance. Late innings," she said.

Trisha took off her backpack and pulled out her poncho. She broke off some of the blue plastic and tied it around the stump of the gatepost. Then she put on her pack and stood between the tall gatepost and the stump.

"The gate was here," she told herself. She looked straight ahead to the northwest. Then she turned and looked to the southeast. "So there must be a path or a road or something. I want—" But her voice began to shake and she wanted to cry. "I want to find the path—any path. Where is it? Help me, Tom. Help me!"

Tom didn't answer. In front of her, all around her, was a field. Beyond this she saw more woods, but no path.

"This is your last chance, Trisha," she said.

Trisha turned and walked northwest. Then she looked back to make sure that she had walked in a straight line. She had, and she looked forward again. There were just more trees, with their branches moving in the wind.

She turned and walked back to the old gatepost and the stump. This time she walked southeast. Woods, nothing but woods. No path. She walked on, trying not to cry.

"What's that?" Tom asked from behind her.

"What?" she replied. "I don't see anything."

"To your left." When she turned round, his finger was pointing over her shoulder.

"That's just an old tree stump," she said. But was it? Or was she afraid to believe that it was a—

"No, I think that it's another post," Tom said.

Trisha pushed through the bushes towards it. And yes, it was another post! A man had put it there.

Now she needed to find the path.

"Please God, help me to find the path," she thought, and she closed her eyes. "Help me in the late innings."

She opened her eyes wide and saw without really looking. Five seconds went by, fifteen seconds, thirty. And then it was there. The shadows all pointing the same way. There were fewer trees and more light. It was an old path.

"I can stay on the path if I don't think about it too much," Trisha told herself, beginning to walk. "If I think about it, it will disappear."

A moment later, she came to another post.

So Trisha started following the posts. They had been put there by a farmer named Elias McCorkle in the year 1905. They marked a trail. Sometimes there were no posts for as far as Trisha could see. But she did not stop to look for them in the grass or bushes. She followed the line of the shadows and the light.

She walked for the rest of that day, with her eyes always following the path. Seven hours later, she came to the edge of another clearing. Three posts went into the middle of it, and part of a gate was still attached to one of them. Beyond it, going south and grown over with grass, was an old road through the woods.

Trisha walked slowly past the gate and onto the road. She started to cry.

"It's a road! I found a road!" she cried. "Thank you, God! Thank you for this road!"

At last she stopped and took off her pack. Then she lay down on the road and looked up at the sky.

———

A few minutes later, Trisha got up. She walked along the road for another hour, until it was almost dark. Off in the west, she heard the sound of thunder. If there was a storm, she needed to get off the road, under the trees, although she would still get wet. But that didn't matter, not now.

She saw something ahead and stopped. It was something else from the world of people—a thing with corners. She moved towards it. It was a truck, or the cab[37] of a truck. It was partly covered with long grass and bushes. There was no glass in the windows of the cab, but there was still a seat inside. Some small animals had eaten part of the seat.

There was more thunder and Trisha saw lightning in the sky. She found a stick and pushed it through the front window of the cab. She hit the seat several times and dust came out through the window spaces. The dust got inside Trisha's mouth and throat and she started coughing. She wasn't going to sleep in the cab, she decided. She didn't want to get more dust inside her and cough for seven or eight hours.

She went a little way into the woods. She sat down under a large tree, ate some nuts and drank some water. She needed more food and water, but she was too tired to worry about it.

———

The night was hot, but Trisha was soon asleep. She woke up

two hours later when cold rain started to fall on her face. Then the thunder crashed over her head and lightning lit up the sky. She jumped up and started running towards the cab with her pack. There was another CRASH! of thunder, and somewhere a tree fell in the forest.

But the Thing was here, and very close!

Trisha came out of the woods to the edge of the road. In a few seconds her clothes were wet through. Her skin was wet under them. She reached the driver's door of the cab and there was more lightning. Trisha saw something standing on the other side of the road, something with black eyes and big pointed ears. It wasn't human, and she didn't think it was an animal. It was the Wasp-God, standing there in the rain, watching her!

"NO!" she screamed, and jumped into the truck cab. "NO, GO AWAY! GO AWAY AND LEAVE ME ALONE!"

Thunder crashed again and the rain hit the cab's roof harder than ever. Trisha hid her head in her arms and rolled over on her side, coughing and shaking. She was still waiting for the Thing to come when she fell asleep again.

When she woke up, it was hot and sunny and the trees seemed greener than before. She could hear the birds singing all around her in the woods.

It was here last night. You saw it. It was waiting for you.

But had she seen it?

You saw it. It came for you, but then you climbed into the truck. It decided to wait a while.

Or maybe she hadn't seen it at all. Maybe it was all a dream. The kind of dream you had when you were half awake and half asleep at the same time.

Trisha got her pack and jumped down from the cab. She started to put the pack on and then stopped. The day was bright and warm and the rain had stopped but there was something wrong.

People could imagine things when they woke up suddenly. But she wasn't imagining this.

During the night, something had made a circle in the leaves and grass around the truck cab. Bushes and small trees had been pulled out of the ground to make the circle.

The God of the Lost had come and drawn a circle around her. It was a message to all the animals in the wood. The message was, "Stay away. She is mine."

11

Something in the Night

Trisha walked along the road all that Sunday. She was very hot in the sun, and very tired. Twice she thought she saw the Thing in the woods, but maybe it was only the sun moving through the trees. She didn't *want* to see it. She didn't want to see those terrible black eyes watching her.

"But it's not going to let me escape," she thought. "And I'm so tired."

She filled her water bottle from the rainwater which remained in pools on the road. The water wasn't very clean, but Trisha didn't care. She was more worried about food.

"After breakfast tomorrow, there'll be no food left," she told herself.

She filled her water bottle from the rainwater which remained in pools in the road.

The road went on and on. About four o'clock in the afternoon, Trisha fell over. She tried to get up, but couldn't. Her legs were shaking and she felt very weak. She took off her pack and ate the last three beechnuts. She was almost sick! She quickly drank some of her water.

"It's Red Sox time," she said aloud, and took out her Walkman.

It took her a long time to find the voice of Joe Castiglione, and he was difficult to hear.

"Garciaparra hits a long high drive to deep center field! It's GONE! Red Sox lead, two to nothing!"

But Trisha was already sleeping. During the fifth inning of the game, something came to the edge of the woods and looked at her. It stood there for a long time. At last it pointed at her with one claw-hand and then went back into the woods again.

When Trisha woke up, it was almost dark. And her Walkman was quiet.

"You fell asleep without switching it off, you stupid girl," she said to herself. "Now the batteries are finished!"

It was like losing her last friend, and she cried. She pushed the radio back into her pack, then put the pack on. It felt heavy, although it was almost empty.

"I'm on a road," she told herself. "That's good. But maybe the stupid road goes on through the woods for another hundred and fifty miles. And maybe there's nothing at the end of the road—just more bushes and another swamp!"

But she began to walk again, slowly and with her head down. After half an hour it was dark and she decided to stop for the night. She sat down on the road and took off her pack. Then she lay down with her head resting on it. She looked at the dark woods to her right.

"You stay away from me," she said aloud.

In the woods, something heard her. It did not reply, but it was there. She could feel it. She drank a little water and then took off her Red Sox cap. She looked for the name on the front. Her father had sent the cap to Fenway Park with a letter to Tom Gordon. The letter asked Tom to sign the cap for Trisha. The letter said that Tom was her favorite player. Tom had signed the cap and sent it back. But now it was wet and dirty like the rest of her clothes, and you couldn't read Tom's signature. It was just a dirty black mark.

———

Trisha woke several times that night, sure that the Thing was there with her. And Tom Gordon spoke to her several times. Once her father spoke to her too. He stood beside her, but when she turned around there was nobody there. More bright meteors fell across the sky.

"Are they real, or are they part of a dream?" she asked herself.

Once, she took out her radio, hoping that the batteries were OK after a rest. But she dropped it into the high grass and couldn't find it. Or maybe she hadn't taken it out of her pack at all. She couldn't be sure. She coughed a lot.

At last the birds began to sing and daylight came through the trees. Trisha opened her eyes and she was surprised to be still alive. She got up slowly. Her head hurt and she saw black spots in front of her eyes. At last the spots went away, but it took her some time to put on her pack. It seemed so heavy.

She looked up and down the road. "Which way was I going?" she asked herself.

Her foot touched something in the grass. It was her Walkman. She picked it up and looked at it stupidly. Was she going to take her pack off again, open it, and put the Walkman back inside? That seemed too hard. It would be easier to move a mountain! But to throw the Walkman away seemed wrong.

Trisha stood for three minutes, looking at the radio.

"Throw it away or keep it? Throw it away or keep it? Decide, Trisha!" she sang.

She started to laugh at herself, but then she began to cough again. The coughing was much worse than before. After a minute, she could feel something warm and wet coming from her mouth. It was blood.

She knew that the blood came from somewhere deep inside her, and it frightened her. "But I can't do anything about it," she told herself.

The sun was coming through the trees on her left, and immediately she realized that she was facing the right way. Slowly, Trisha started moving again.

"Today is probably my last chance," she thought. "Maybe this morning is my last chance. Maybe I'll be too weak to walk by this afternoon."

She looked down and saw her Walkman in her hand. She stopped. She slowly and carefully fixed it to her jeans. She was trying to decide what to do with the headphones when she heard several small explosions. She jumped and cried out.

But she knew that sound. It was a car backfiring[38], or maybe a truck. There was another road ahead! A bigger road. A road which people used!

She wanted to run, but knew that she was too weak. She

began to walk, listening for the sounds of more cars or trucks. There was nothing. After an hour she began to think she had imagined the sound. It had seemed real, but—

She came to the top of a hill and looked down. She began coughing again, and more blood came from her mouth. But Trisha did not notice it. Below her, the road she was standing on joined another, wider road.

Trisha walked slowly down and stood on the new road. It went east and west. She turned west because her head was hurting and she didn't want to walk towards the bright sun. It was the right thing to do. Four miles away, Route 96 ran through the woods. A few cars and many more trucks used this road.

She began to move forwards again, feeling stronger. Forty-five minutes later she heard a sound that she recognized.

"Don't be stupid. It can't be!" she told herself.

But she was right. It was the sound of traffic on a road. It was far away, but it was certainly the sound of traffic.

Trisha began to cry. "Please let the sound be real," she said. "Please God, let it be real."

Suddenly, a louder noise came from behind her. Was it the sound of tree branches breaking? And then the sound of something falling—a small tree?

"It's coming," Trisha thought. "Something is in its way. But it's coming for me. The God of the Lost is coming for me."

Slowly, she turned around.

12

Time to Close

It came from the trees on the left side of the road. "Is that all?" Trisha thought. "Is that all it is?"

It was a North American black bear. It was holding a broken branch in its mouth, between its great teeth.

The bear came to the middle of the road. At first it stayed on all four of its feet, but then it stood up on its back legs. When it did, Trisha saw that it was not a black bear at all. It really was the God of the Lost, and it had come for her.

The God looked at her with black eyes that were not eyes at all, but only eye-holes. It bit the branch into two pieces, making a sound like bones breaking. That was the sound that Trisha's arm would make when the Thing bit it. The Thing chopped the pieces of the branch.

Now it was no more than six feet away from her.

It had come for her!

The God of the Lost called to her. *Run from me! This bear's body that I have today is slow. Run! Perhaps I'll let you live.*

"Yes, run!" she told herself. And then she heard the cold voice. *You can't run. You can only just stand up.*

The Thing that wasn't really a bear stood looking at her. It was seven feet tall. Its head was in the sky and its claws held the earth. Bugs flew round its head and around its eyes. It told her what she already knew. *I killed the deer. I watched you and I made my circle around you. Run from me.*

The woods were silent around them.

"It's time to close," Trisha thought. "I know what I must do."

She pulled her cap low over her eyes. It was the way Tom Gordon wore his cap. She turned to the right so that her left leg pointed at the Thing like a bear. Then she looked into its eye-holes.

"This is it!" Joe Castiglione said in Trisha's head. "The time has come. Wait for it, everybody!"

"Come on then," Trisha called to the Thing. She pulled the Walkman from her jeans and held it behind her back. "Come on!"

The bear dropped its stick and put its front feet back on the ground. Then it moved towards her. It was walking, but it was moving fast. Trisha could see its teeth, and she could hear a buzzing sound coming from its mouth. Wasps. The thing was full of wasps.

Run! Run, it's your last chance! The voice in her head was telling her what to do. But she knew that it was wrong. Waiting, being calm, like Tom Gordon—*that* was her last chance.

Trisha put her hands together. Now the Walkman was a baseball. There was no Fenway Park crowd, no cheering. There was only Trisha, the hot morning sun, and a Thing that looked like a bear. A Thing that looked like a bear on the outside and was full of wasps on the inside.

"No! I won't run," she thought.

The Thing stopped in front of her. There were no eyes, only two circles full of bugs. Its mouth was open and she saw that it was full of wasps.

She didn't move. Let it wait. Soon she would make her pitch, but let it wait.

The Thing smelled around her face. Bugs crawled in and out of its nose. Its face was changing all the time. Trisha saw the faces of her teachers and friends. She saw the faces of her parents and brother. The Thing had the face of dangerous strangers. And it smelled of death.

The bear stood up on its back legs again, and then it stretched out a claw. The claw missed Trisha's her face by several inches. She didn't move. She didn't look at its face, she looked at its stomach.

It seemed to speak to her. *Look at me.*

"No."

Look at me!

Slowly, Trisha looked up into the Thing's empty black eyes. She understood then. It was going to kill her now.

But it was time to close.

Without thinking about it, Trisha moved her left foot back against her right. She was moving like Tom Gordon. She had watched Tom do this a hundred times on TV. When she stepped forward again and put her right hand up to her right ear and then behind it, the bear stepped back. It made a surprised sound—a loud grunt. Wasps came out of its mouth.

And then a Trisha heard the sound of a gunshot.

————

The man in the woods that morning was the first human being to see Trisha McFarland in nine days. His name was Travis Herrick and he was hunting deer.

"Thank God she didn't move, or the bear would have killed her," he told the police later. "At first I couldn't shoot. She was too near it—I was afraid of hitting her. Then she moved. She had something in her hand and she started to throw it—like a baseball throw. That surprised the bear, and it moved back. And that's when I shot it."

But it was time to close.

———

Trisha heard the gunshot and saw one of the Thing's ears fly away from its head. She also saw the blood flying into the air. And at that moment she saw that the Thing was only a bear again. Or maybe it had been a bear all the time.

But she knew that it had not.

She threw the Walkman and it hit the bear between the eyes.

"Strike three!" she screamed.

At the sound of her voice, the bear turned and ran away. There was another gunshot, but the bear disappeared into the woods. Trisha turned and saw a man running towards her. He was carrying a gun high above his head. She wasn't surprised to see that he was wearing a Red Sox shirt. "Every man in New England has at least one Red Sox shirt," she thought.

"Girl!" the man screamed. "Are you all right? That was a bear! Are you really OK?"

"Did you see?" she said. "Did you see me throw? I got it. I got the save!"

And then she fainted.

———

She was in the woods again. She came to a clearing. She knew the clearing. Tom Gordon was standing in the middle of it by the gatepost.

"I've already had this dream," she thought. But she and Tom were here again, in the clearing.

"Tom?" she said. "I closed."

"I know," Tom said. "You were very good."

"How much of it was real?" she asked him.

"All of it," he replied.

"I was stupid to get off the path, wasn't I?" she said.

86

Tom looked surprised. Then he smiled.

"What path?" he said.

"Trisha?"

That was a woman's voice, coming from behind her. It was her mother's voice. But why would her mother be out here in the woods?

"She probably doesn't hear you," said another woman's voice.

Trisha turned. The woods were getting darker. Shapes were moving. The Wasp-God was coming back. Then she realized that she was dreaming. She turned back to Tom, but he wasn't there.

"Look," her mother said to someone. "Her lips are moving."

"Trisha?" That was Pete's voice. "Are you awake?"

She opened her eyes. She was in a hospital bed. Standing by the bed were her father, her mother, her brother. Behind them was a nurse.

"Trisha," Mom said. She was crying. "Oh, Trisha!"

Pete was crying, too.

Trisha tried to smile, but her mouth was too heavy to move. She moved her eyes instead and saw her Red Sox cap on the chair by her bed. "Dad," she tried to say, but she only coughed. It hurt.

"Don't try to talk, Trisha," the nurse said. "You're a sick girl. You've got pneumonia[39]."

Her mother was sitting on the bed beside her now. Pete stood next to her, still crying. Beside Pete and next to the chair, stood her father. This time, Trisha didn't try to speak, but she made the word "Dad" with her mouth.

He saw it and moved forward. "What?" he said quickly.

"It's time to go now," the nurse said. "She needs to sleep."

Mom stood up. "We love you, Trisha. Thank God you're safe. Larry, let's—"

But Trisha's father moved nearer to her. "What is it, Trisha?" he said. "What do you want?"

She moved her eyes to the chair, to his face, and back to the chair. He smiled and picked up the cap. He tried to put it on her head but she put up her hand. Then she opened the fingers. Closed them. Opened them.

He understood. "OK," he said, smiling. And he put the cap in her hand, then kissed her fingers. Trisha began to cry, silently.

"OK," the nurse said. "Now you all really must leave."

Trisha looked at the nurse and shook her head.

"What?" the nurse asked her. "What do you want?"

Trisha slowly put the cap into her other hand. Her father watched her. She was tired. Soon she would sleep. But not yet. She reached across her body with her right hand, watching her father because he would understand.

Trisha touched the cap, then pointed the first finger on her right hand up at the ceiling. Larry McFarland smiled. He understood.

Trisha closed her eyes. And slept.

Game over!

Points for Understanding

1

"Those two don't even remember that I'm here," Trisha says to herself. What does she mean?

2

Why doesn't Trisha want to walk around the huge fallen tree?

3

Why does Trisha follow the stream down into the valley?

4

What does Larry McFarland believe in?

5

Trisha's divorced parents are sleeping in the same bed in the hotel. Is this important? What do you think?

6

Why does Trisha decide to try to cross the swamp?

7

Trisha thinks about Tom Gordon. How does this help her?

8

Trisha had been dreaming about the three people with robes. Why does she have that particular dream? Make some guesses.

9

Why doesn't Trisha want to think about eating the fish?

10

Why is Trisha happy when she finds the first gatepost?

11

Why does Trisha cry when her Walkman won't work?

12

Why does Trisha throw her Walkman at the bear?

A Guide to Pronunciation

Trisha McFarland	/ˌtrɪʃə mækˈfɑːlənd/
Eddie Rayburn	/ˌediː ˈreɪbɜːn/
Pepsi Robichaud	/ˌpepsiː ˈrəʊbɪʃəʊ/
Joe Castiglione	/ˌdʒəʊ ˈkəstɪglɪˈəʊniː/
Jerry Trupiano	/ˌdʒeriː truːpiːˈɑːnəʊ/
Tino Martinez	/ˌtiːnəʊ mɑːˈtiːnez/
Veritek	/ˈveərətek/
Francis Raymond Mazzerole	/ˌfrænsɪs ˌreɪmənd mætsəˈrəʊliː/
Elias McCorkle	/əˌlɪəs mæˈkɔːkɪl/
Garciaparra	/ˌgɑːsɪəˈpærə/
Darryl Strawberry	/ˌdærɪl ˈstrɔːberiː/
Travis Herrick	/ˌtrævɪs ˈheərɪk/

Glossary

1   **pee**—*to pee* (page 9)
    an expression used by children that means, "to pass urine".
    Adults sometimes use this word too.
2   **custody**—*to get custody* (page 9)
    when two people end their marriage by getting divorced, one of
    them usually *gets custody* of their children. The children then
    live with that parent. They also visit, or receive visits from, the
    other parent.
3   **Pete's Compuworld** (page 10)
    Pete's friends have given him a name that sounds like the
    names of some large stores in the U.S. In these stores, you can
    buy every kind of computer equipment. Pete's friends are mak-
    ing a joke about his interest in everything to do with computers.
4   **canoe trip** (page 10)
    a *trip* is a journey which you make for pleasure. A *canoe* is a kind
    of small, narrow boat, which is pointed at both ends.
5   **Appalachian Trial** (page 10)
    a long route for walkers in the eastern U.S. Part of the
    Appalachian Trail runs through the Appalachian Mountains.
6   **bugs** (page 10)
    small insects. You can spray your skin with a chemical, con-
    tained in *a bug spray*. This keeps the insects from biting you.
7   **poncho** (page 11)
    a garment which you wear over your shoulders. Originally it was
    a kind of square blanket with a hole which you put your head
    through. But Trisha's poncho is made of plastic, and is for pro-
    tection against rain.
8   **backpack/pack** (page 11)
    a small waterproof bag which you wear on your back. You use it
    to carry things when you are walking or climbing.
9   **ravine** (page 12)
    a very narrow valley with steep sides.
10 **hikers** (page 14)
    people who walk for pleasure.
11 **diverged** (page 14)
    two things which start at the same place and then move apart
    are said to *diverge*.

12 **mosquitoes** (page 15)
a *mosquito* is a small flying insect which bites people or animals and drinks their blood.

13 **Shut up!** (page 15)
an impolite expression that means, "Be quiet!"

14 **checkerberries** (page 17)
the *checkerberry bush* is also called wintergreen. It is a small green bush which has bright red berries—*checkerberries*.

15 **suntan lotion** (page 17)
a kind of oil which you rub on your skin to stop the sun from burning it on hot days.

16 **Twinkies** (page 17)
small sweet cakes that you can buy in a store.

17 **Forest Service** (page 19)
a department of the government which takes care of the forests and woodlands. *Game wardens* control the way that people hunt animals in these areas. Animals which are hunted are called *game* animals.

18 **Walkman** (page 22)
a kind of small tape-cassette player which you carry with you and listen to through headphones. It is powered by batteries. Trisha's *Walkman* contains a radio as well as a cassette player.

19 **announcer** (page 23)
a person who speaks between radio programs, to link them together.

20 **wasp** (page 23)
a small flying insect with a black and yellow body. *Wasps* can sting you painfully. A wasp's sting often makes your flesh swell.

21 **soothe** (page 23)
to do something which reduces pain in a part of your body is to *soothe* that part. You can also soothe someone's worry or fear.

22 **search party** (page 26)
a group of people who go to search for someone who is lost.

23 **walkie-talkies** (page 26)
kinds of small radio communication instruments, with microphones and loud speakers, that two people use to speak to each other.

24 **bull horns** (page 26)
electronic instruments for making a voice louder. They look like a kind of horn. You put one end of a *bull horn* to your lips and

93

speak through it. Your voice is amplified, so that people far away can hear it.

24 **closer** (page 28)

a baseball player who is always able to score points at important times and help his team win baseball games. NOTE: this is pronounced like "dozer".

25 **commentators** (page 28)

people who give a continuous description of a game on radio or television.

26 **curveball** (page 30)

when a baseball pitcher throws the ball and it changes its path before it reaches the batter, this is a *curveball*. NOTE: other baseball words used in this part of the book are given in the note on page 5.

27 **numb** (page 33)

if you lose the feeling in a part of your body for a short time, that part has become *numb*.

28 **swamp** (page 40)

an area of land where the ground is full of water. Usually the water covers some but not all of the ground.

29 **hummocks** (page 41)

small raised areas of ground.

30 **beavers** (page 45)

animals with brown fur, wide flat tails and very strong teeth. *Beavers* live on both land and in water. They use their teeth to cut down trees. They use these trees for building their houses and for blocking streams.

31 **police record** (page 51)

if you commit a crime, the police keep a record of this crime and your address so that they can find you in future.

32 **hung up**—to hang up (page 51)

an expression which means, "to end a phone call".

33 **kidnapped** (page 54)

if someone is taken away suddenly and roughly, and kept somewhere against their wishes, that person has been *kidnapped*.

34 **meteor** (page 62)

an object which falls towards the Earth from space and burns up. As a *meteor* burns, it makes a bright line in the night sky.

35 **marsh** (page 66)

an area of wet land, from which the water cannot escape.

36 *cab* (page 74)

the part of a truck where the driver and passengers sit.

37 *backfiring* (page 80)

if the engine of a car or a truck is not working properly, it often makes very loud sounds, like small explosions. This is called *backfiring*.

38 *pneumonia* (page 87)

a serious illness of the lungs which makes breathing difficult.

Published by Macmillan Heinemann ELT
Between Towns Road, Oxford OX4 3PP
Macmillan Heinemann ELT is an imprint of
Macmillan Publishers Limited
Companies and representatives throughout the world
Heinemann is a registered trademark of Harcourt Education, used under licence.

ISBN 1–405072–94–6
EAN 978–1–405072–94–6

This retold version by John Escott for Macmillan Readers
First published 2002

This edition first published 2005

Illustrated by Annabel Large
Original cover template design by Jackie Hill
Cover photography by Corbis

Printed in Thailand

2009 2008 2007 2006 2005
10 9 8 7 6 5 4 3 2 1